The Little Shot
Growth

By Tasha Eizinger
Illustrated by Miranda Meeks

GROUND TRUTH PRESS

NASHUA, NEW HAMPSHIRE

The Little Shot Series, Book Three

Published by

GROUND TRUTH PRESS
P. O. Box 7313
Nashua, NH 03060-7313

Illustrations and Cover Design: Miranda Meeks

Editor: Bonnie Lyn Smith

Technical Editor: Melissa Hicks

PowerV® is a trademark owned by, and use of the PowerV® words is under a license from, MetaMetrics, Inc. All rights reserved.

The Little Shot® is a registered trademark of The Little Shot, LLC.

Trade paperback ISBN-13: 978-1-7359307-5-6
Trade paperback ISBN-10: 1-7359307-5-X

First printing, 2021
Printed in the United States of America

Publisher's Cataloging-In-Publication Data
(Prepared by The Donohue Group, Inc.)

Names: Eizinger, Tasha, author. | Meeks, Miranda, illustrator.
Title: The Little Shot. Growth / by Tasha Eizinger ; illustrated by Miranda Meeks.
Other Titles: Growth
Description: Nashua, New Hampshire : Ground Truth Press, [2021] | Series: The Little Shot series ; book 3 | Includes keyword index. | Interest age level: 004-009. | Interest grade level: K-3. | Summary: "Life has become comfortable for Little Shot. She is successful and thinks she is enjoying it. However, her parents challenge her to grow so she can become her best. With the help of her mentor, Little Shot decides to teach another star how to become a Big Shot, a shooting star. She realizes life is more exciting when you are growing!"--Provided by publisher.
Identifiers: ISBN 9781735930756 (trade paperback) | ISBN 173593075X (trade paperback)
Subjects: LCSH: Stars--Juvenile fiction. | Maturation (Psychology)--Juvenile fiction. | Meteors--Juvenile fiction. | Teaching--Juvenile fiction. | CYAC: Stars--Fiction. | Maturation (Psychology)--Fiction. | Meteors--Fiction. | Teaching--Fiction.
Classification: LCC PZ7.1.E59 Lg 2021 | DDC [E]--dc23

Library of Congress Control Number: 2021913903

This book is dedicated to my sweet Little Shots and to all the Little Shots!

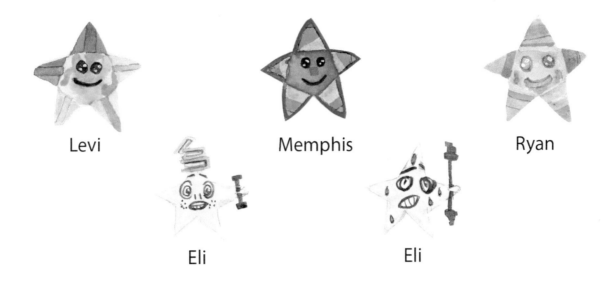

Levi

Eli

Memphis

Eli

Ryan

Thank you to the Little Shots who decorated a star featured in this book!

*****

Thank you to everyone who has challenged us
to grow outside of our comfort zone.

Beta Readers:
Christine Carter, Judy Edwards, Lisa Trimble, Taylor Edwards, and Marilyn Peters

Beta Viewers:
Priya Evans, Suzana Rodriguez-Griffin, Phyllis Anne Taylor, and Heidi Witte

"Great job, everyone!" Little Shot high-fived the other Big Shots, also known as shooting stars. Little Shot had become comfortable with her Big Shot success. When something didn't feel quite right, it was easy to ignore the feeling.

"Hey, Mom and Dad! Everything went well again!"

"Wonderful! Your consistency has created success. It's time to push yourself and do something out of your comfort zone," said her mom.

"What do you mean?"

"You have gotten comfortable with your success so you haven't grown."

"But, I am taller."

Her mom smiled, "Yes, you are, but this type of growth happens inside."

"Do you remember how you felt becoming a Big Shot?"
asked her dad.

"I was nervous and excited. I worked so hard!"

"We loved watching you develop into a Big Shot. We
know it wasn't easy for you because we saw you working
outside of your comfort zone.

Growth and becoming your best happen when you challenge yourself,"
said her dad.

"Little Shot, we have loved watching you develop your confidence and abilities. It's time to challenge yourself to see what more you can learn. Life is more fun when you're growing," said her mom.

"Thanks, Mom and Dad. I'm going for a walk to think."

On her walk, she saw her friends. Some of them were content where they were. The others, who were challenging themselves, seemed more excited about life.

Maybe she should visit with her grandma.

"Hey, Grandma!"

"Hi, Little Shot!"

"Grandma, do you think life is better when you are growing?"

"Yes," she said with a knowing smile. "I'm still learning and growing and will never stop."

"It's time for a new goal!" Little Shot exclaimed.

Being a big dreamer, her grandma's eyes twinkled with delight.
"Who can you ask about the next best step for a Big Shot?"
"My mentors!"

"Yes, please let me know what they say. I will always be rooting
for you!"

Little Shot felt alive with nervous excitement again. She found her favorite mentor who always happily guided her.

"Did you ever get comfortable and stop pushing yourself?" asked Little Shot.

"Absolutely! It's an easy thing to do. I learned that teaching someone else how to become a Big Shot helped me grow."

"Little Shot, life is good when you achieve your own goal.
Life is fulfilling when you help someone else."

"Will you help me?"

"Yes!"

"I don't want to mess up someone else's Big Shot dream."

"Remember, Little Shot, someone else's success is not your responsibility. You can offer to help them, but they have to do the hard work."

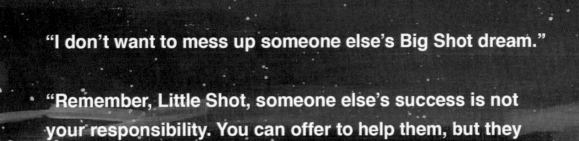

Little Shot found a star who was ready and willing to learn. She realized it was more fun challenging herself while teaching another star how to become a Big Shot. Finally, after hard work and many failed attempts, Little Shot knew the little star was ready to soar.

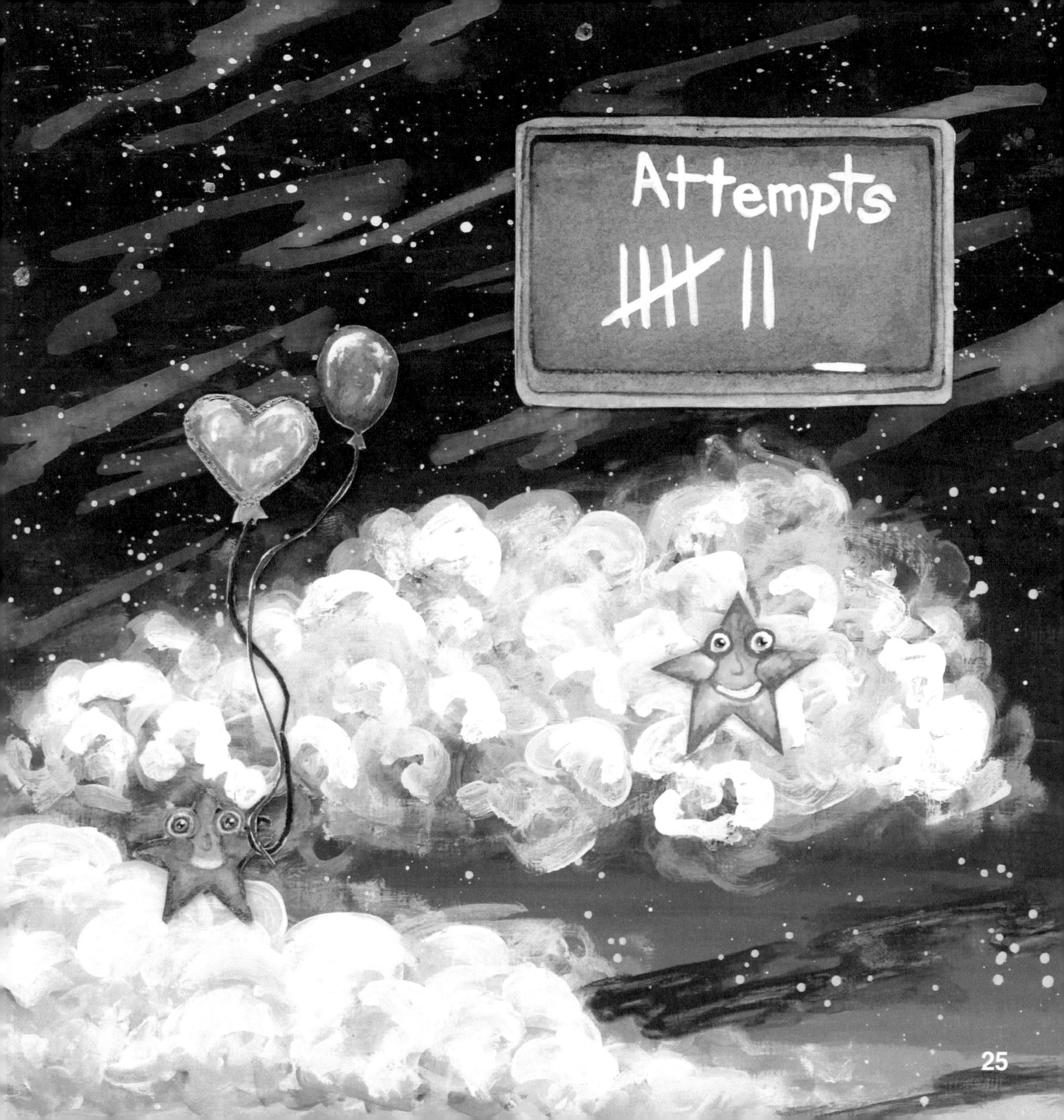
Attempts

"You've got this!" she encouraged him as they lined up with the other Big Shots. "You ready?"

"Yes!" he nervously shouted.

3... 2... 1...

Little Shot felt alive! Growing herself by helping someone else made life more fulfilling. Little Shot looked down and saw someone looking up at them while making a wish upon a brand-new shooting star.

Courage

Growth

My Big Shot Journal

1.) Consistency = Success
2.) Push yourself = Growth
3.) Become my best.
4.) Growth is exciting!
5.) Teach someone else.

Humility

New Goals!

Hope

~~Comfort Zone~~

Life has become comfortable for Little Shot. She is successful and thinks she is enjoying it. However, her parents challenge her to grow so she can become her best. With the help of her mentor, Little Shot decides to teach another star how to become a Big Shot, a shooting star. She realizes life is more exciting when she is growing! Follow Little Shot's journey as she learns about growth.

LEXILE
WORDLISTS

Little Shot teamed up with the Lexile® PowerV® Vocabulary API & Service to offer this enriching vocabulary list. Dive right in and see how many Lexile® PowerV® words you can find in this book. Read along with a partner and tell them what each word means.

Achieve	**Delight**	**Offer**
Comfort	**Develop**	**Responsibility**
Confidence	**Growth**	**Soar**
Consistency	**Ignore**	**Success**
Content	**Mentor**	

CPSIA information can be obtained
at www.ICGtesting.com
Printed in the USA
BVRC090745301021
620335BV00002B/12